Priscilla

AND THE GREAT SANTA SEARCH

by Nathaniel Hobbie ❧•❧ Illustrated by Jocelyn Hobbie

LITTLE, BROWN AND COMPANY
Books for Young Readers
New York   Boston

Little, Brown and Company

Hachette Book Group USA
237 Park Avenue, New York, NY 10017 • Visit our Web site at www.lb-kids.com

First Edition: October 2008

Library of Congress Cataloging-in-Publication Data

Hobbie, Nathaniel.
Priscilla and the great Santa search / by Nathaniel Hobbie ;
illustrated by Jocelyn Hobbie.
p. cm.
Summary: Priscilla and her best friend Bettina set out on
cross-country skis to find the North Pole and the real Santa Claus.
ISBN 978-0-316-11331-1
[1. Stories in rhyme. 2. Adventure and adventurers--Fiction. 3. Santa
Claus--Fiction. 4. North Pole--Fiction.] I. Hobbie, Jocelyn, ill. II.
Title.
PZ8.3.H655Pqg 2008
[E]--dc22
2008010347

10 9 8 7 6 5 4 3 2 1

TWP
Printed in Singapore

The world was wrapped in a blanket of white,
Everything soft and sparkling bright.
It was coming up quick — the best time of the year.
That magical season all children hold dear.

Some kids were busy dodging snowballs,
    Or lined up to see Santa out at the malls.
Others made lists with pencil and pad,
    Hoping they hadn't been *horribly* bad.

Dear Santa

WISH LIST

Priscilla, of course, was out on the ice
Trying to master the triple-toe splice,
When Bettina, whose skating was really clip-clopping,
Suggested they pack it in and go shopping.

Outside the Precious Princess Boutique,
Christmas fever was reaching its peak.
Shoppers buzzed like a hive full of bees,
Balancing boxes stacked up high as trees.

Carolers sang at the tops of their lungs,
Or teetered tiptoe getting ornaments hung.
The air was awaft with puddings and cakes,
But wherever they turned stood Santa Claus FAKES.

SANTA

"Look at that one," Priscilla noted with wonder.
"His beard's coming off. What a terrible blunder."
"And that one's too skinny. Who is *he* fooling?"
"These Santas don't pass." That was their ruling.

"Imagine meeting the *real* Mr. Claus.
That'd be amazing," Priscilla said with applause.

Then it hit her like a sock full of coal.
"We can!" she cried. "He lives at the North Pole."

That night Bettina just *had* to sleep over.
With her, of course, came Mirabelle Clover.
Those girls were up giggling way past lights-out.
But that's what planning a trip's all about.

North Pole

When the midnight hour was finally at hand
They drifted away into sugarplum land,
And dreamed, all cozy and curled up in bed,
Of the real Santa Claus and their adventure ahead.

Come morning, those girls arose with the sun
And fueled up on cocoa and cinnamon buns.
Then straightaway they started to pack.
So much was needed, not a second to slack.

Snow pants, hats, mittens, and coats—
Little pink candies for soothing sore throats.
They whipped up a stack of PB&J's,
And a thermos of cocoa — very gourmet;
Camera, radio, "and sunscreen, too, please,"
Compass, map, and cross-country skis.

Take only the basics. That was their creed.
  Though there's no telling what two girls might need.
Bettina's dog, Fluffball, was begging to go.
  Old Fluffers, they figured, was made for the snow.

The air was nose-nipping, but the sky crystal-clear.
Said P, "Perfect weather." Said B, "Yes, my dear."
They strapped on their skis without further ado,
And pointed them north to find you know who.

Fluffball the Brave courageously led,
  And across the wintry wilds they sped.
Sometimes they stopped to study the map,
  Gulp down some cocoa, or tighten a strap.
Sometimes they pretended to be in a movie,
  Posing for pictures and acting all groovy.

The north country creatures were quite a surprise.
Like the Snowball Bunny — what a disguise!
Or the Blue Blubber Bird, who uses its wings
Mostly for pointing while laughing at things.
The Abominable Snowgirl would be a real scare
If she wasn't so busy always grooming her hair.

At ten degrees north they met an odd little man
    Who called himself Jan of the Faraway Clan.
Bundled in furs, and scratching at fleas,
    He had a strange smell, like ripening cheese.

REST ✦ STOP

COCO

NORTH POLE

Jan stood pointing his mitt to the west.
"Hear my words now, for Jan does not jest.
Behold the blackness beginning to form.
Ye must turn back! Fear the fifty-year storm!"

"Turn back? No way!" Those girls set a goal.
They wouldn't turn back. They would reach the North Pole.

Soon the stern sky billowed with clouds,
   And snow cascaded in great sweeping shrouds.
But then up ahead they could see plain
   The pole that possessed that most honored name.

THE
North
Pole!

The North Pole! There it stood, straight and true!
But as for old Santa, there wasn't a clue.
No sign of elves, no workshop, no sleigh.
It was a bit disappointing, so late in the day.

And still the storm worsened. The hot cocoa froze.
Icicles dangled at the end of each nose.

The radio weatherman proved Jan had been right.
"...a class seven squall at the North Pole tonight..."

Well, Priscilla's upbeat and Bettina is, too.
They kept up their smiles. What else could they do?
But they had to get going — get out of there quick!
Though not before posing for one final pic.

Homeward that hasty group set their sights,
  Eager for the warmth of town's twinkling lights.
On Main Street they heard the dinner bells chime
  And called out together, "Yippee! Right on time."

After three servings of Christmas Eve stew,
  Their sapped-away strength began to renew.
With two cups of milk and cookies to dip,
  They slipped off to look at the pics of their trip.

"And what did you find in the north zone?"
    Bettina asked, holding a pretend microphone.
"The animals," said Priscilla, acting the part,
    "Are right at the top of the oddity chart.
As for Kris Kringle, we had rotten luck.
    If only that storm hadn't run us amuck."

"But wait!" she cried out. "What is this?
 Here in the background. Something we missed."
"Zoom in," said Bettina. "Let's get a look."
 And there, what they saw could not be mistook.

Though it was blurry and fuzzy and gray,
    They made out eight reindeer pulling a sleigh.
And driving the sleigh, although very dim,
    Was right there to see, "Look! Look, it's *HIM*!"

"Santa," they gasped together with awe,
Almost unable to believe what they saw.

"We were so close! He was right there!"
"The *real* Santa Claus up-up in the air!"

It was all so astounding, an incredible sight.
  What a perfectly magical Christmas Eve night!
There's no better feeling than Santa can bring.
  "Merry Christmas to all!" they started to sing.

That night as Priscilla was all snuggled in,
　　Pulling the covers right up to her chin,
She could imagine Santa so clear,
　　And knew he was coming, as he does every year.